About the Author

Stephen J. Alexander was born in Shrewsbury, Shropshire in 1973. He has been a teacher since 1996 and has had the privilege of working with some very creative and interesting people over the years as a teacher of English in London, Girona, Catalonia and Geneva, Switzerland. He is a frequent visitor to Haute-Savoie in France as this is where his wife is from. Laura Coppolaro is a professional illustrator from Cambridgeshire.

Peter and the Dwarf Planets

Stephen J. Alexander

Peter and the Dwarf Planets

Olympia Publishers
London

www.olympiapublishers.com
OLYMPIA PAPERBACK EDITION

ISBN: 978-1-78830-141-1

First Published in 2018

Olympia Publishers
60 Cannon Street
London
EC4N 6NP
Printed in Great Britain

For Rubén and Lucie. Always follow your dreams!
From papa.

"The next thing there is 'PLUTO,'" said daddy.
"She's very far away,

She's very cold and icy,
So not a place to stay."

"I like that name" said Peter.
"What is Pluto? Why's it there?"

"It's called a DWARF PLANET," answered daddy,
"We can go there if you dare!"

"Oh, yes please," said Pete
As he lay there in his bed.
He snuggled next to daddy
But not to rest his head...

As Peter started dreaming
He floated up to space,
Picked up in daddy's spaceship
His journey gathered pace!

They shot past MARS with its big red glow
And Peter smiled with glee
As daddy dodged the asteroids,
The next thing they did see...

"In amongst this rocky field," said daddy
"we must hold on tight.
And look out very carefully for 'CERES' on our right!"

On they raced right through the darkness of our solar system:
First Jupiter, then Saturn's rings.
To blink they would have missed them.

Whooshing past the two ice-giants.
First Uranus, then Neptune.
Peter smiled a happy smile,
and daddy was smiling too.

For daddy knew what to expect.
He'd been here many times before.
As Peter sat up starry eyed.
And Pluto is what he saw!

The spaceship circled Pluto
so Peter could surely see how BEAUTIFUL a thing
A dwarf planet could really be.

Peter's dream voyage was at an end,
as he fell into a deep and happy slumber.
But daddy's journey carried on.
He had to know the number...

...of dwarf planets. There are five that we know of.
But maybe there are hundreds.

Daddy flew on through deepest space.
To see what he could plunder.

First, **HAUMEA,** like a giant Easter Egg or a brown baked bean.
Then, **MAKEMAKE,** very small, dark brown in colour and ever so serene.
And finally there came **ERIS**, the biggest of the lot.
But so far from our planet, Earth, to us, a small white dot.

In the morning at the breakfast table.
Between milk and cereal, toast and jam,
Peter asked his daddy if they could go past Pluto.
And hatch another plan.

Then daddy whispered close to him,
"Yes, if that is what you want to do,

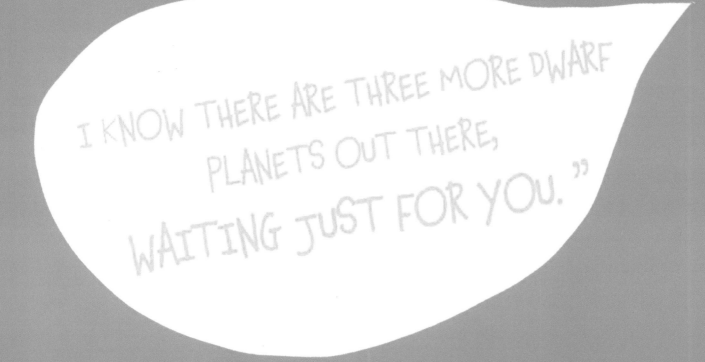

I KNOW THERE ARE THREE MORE DWARF PLANETS OUT THERE, WAITING JUST FOR YOU."

CPSIA information can be obtained at www.ICGtesting.com
Printed in the USA
BVIW121321210720
583810BV00014B/227